lullaby raft

NAOMI SHIHAB NYE

illustrated by

VIVIENNE FLESHER

Simon & Schuster
Books for Young Readers

SIMON AND SCHUSTER BOOKS FOR YOUNG READERS

An imprint of Simon and Schuster Children's Publishing Division

1230 Avenue of the Americas, New York, New York 10020

Text copyright © 1997 by Naomi Shihab Nye

Illustrations copyright © 1997 by Vivienne Flesher

Musical arrangement and lyrics © 1997 by Naomi Shihab Nye

Book design by Heather Wood. The text for this book is set in Barmeno.

Printed and bound in Hong Kong by South China Printing Co. (1988) Ltd.

1   3   5   7   9   10   8   6   4   2

First Edition

Library of Congress Cataloging-in-Publication Data

Nye, Naomi Shihab.

Lullaby raft / by Naomi Shihab; illustrated by Vivienne Flesher. — 1st ed.

p.   cm.

Summary : When the sun goes down, Mama sings a lullaby

which tells of animals getting ready for the night.

ISBN 0-689-80521-7

[1. Animals–Fiction. 2. Night–Fiction. 3. Lullabies.] I. Flesher, Vivienne, ill. II. Title.

PZ7.N976Lu   1996   [E]–dc20   96-22425

Thanks to Sharda Brody for her long friendship,

and thank you to Paul B. Janeczko for his good advice. N.S.N.

• A Note about the Art •

Vivienne Flesher's chalk pastel drawings were created on Reeves BFK paper.

To Miriam Allwardt Shihab and Madison and Michael Nye

N.S.N.

To my friend Ward Schumaker & my dumpling Alfred

V.F.

My mama sings me a lullaby
When the sun goes down

My mama sings me a lullaby all my own
And I dream of her hands
And the years I'll live alone
My mama sings me a lullaby
All my own

My chicken sleeps with her head tucked low
On the sill beside my bed
My chicken hums with her head tucked low
Inside my room

And I tell her what I know
And she tells me in return
My chicken chirps with her wings tucked low
Her nighttime tune

My bunny climbs into my drawer
Where the socks are soft and rolled
My bunny holds her secret note
No one can hear

When her ears are drooping down
And her paws are curled around
My bunny huddles in a mound
To disappear

My turtle lives inside her walls
Where the air feels safe and warm
My turtle folds inside herself
To wait for light

She likes to be alone
With her sand and quiet stone
My turtle learns a single note
To hold all night

My lizard licks the darkness clean
In the leaves outside my room
My lizard zips the shadows free
From the quiet town

He was busy all day long
But the night gives back his song
My lizard sips the sweetest tune
From the sleepy ground

The moon will float like a little rowboat
On the river of the sky
The moon will float like a little rowboat
To the other side

The stars will drift and gently soar
Till morning comes and they climb on board
The moon will float like a little rowboat
Without an oar

hen the life goes round and
The baby grows tall
Who will sing us down to sleep?
When the life goes round and the moon has clouds
Will our dreams still rise?

When the day feels short and the night feels wide
Little stars go run and hide
I'll make me a lullaby raft to ride
To the other side

I'll make me a lullaby raft to ride
To the other side

LULLABY RAFT

My ma - ma sings me a lul - la - by When the sun goes
down My ma - ma sings me a lul - la - by all my own
And I _____ dream of her hands And the years I'll live a -
lone My ma - ma sings me a lul - la - by All my own

VERSE 2

My chicken sleeps with her head tucked low
On the sill beside my bed
My chicken hums with her head tucked low
Inside my room
And I tell her what I know
And she tells me in return
My chicken chirps with her wings tucked low
Her nighttime tune

VERSE 3

My bunny climbs into my drawer
Where the socks are soft and rolled
My bunny holds her secret note
No one can hear
When her ears are drooping down
And her paws are curled around
My bunny huddles in a mound
To disappear

VERSE 4

My turtle lives inside her walls
Where the air feels safe and warm
My turtle folds inside herself
To wait for light
She likes to be alone
With her sand and quiet stone
My turtle learns a single note
To hold all night

VERSE 5

My lizard licks the darkness clean
In the leaves outside my room
My lizard zips the shadows free
From the quiet town
He was busy all day long
But the night gives back his song
My lizard sips the sweetest tune
From the sleepy ground

VERSE 6

The moon will float like a little rowboat
On the river of the sky
The moon will float like a little rowboat
To the other side
The stars will drift and gently soar
Till morning comes and they climb on board
The moon will float like a little rowboat
Without an oar

VERSE 7

When the life goes round and
The baby grows tall
Who will sing us down to sleep?
When the life goes round and the moon has clouds
Will our dreams still rise?
When the day feels short and the night feels wide
Little stars go run and hide
I'll make me a lullaby raft to ride
To the other side